THE CREEPY CLASSICS

CHILDREN'S COLLECTION

Dados Internacionais de Catalogação na Publicação (CIP) de acordo com ISBD

W453i Wells, H. G.
The invisible man / H. G. Wells. - Jandira, SP : W. Books, 2025.
128 p. ; 12,80cm x 19,80cm. - (Classics).

ISBN: 978-65-5294-197-8

1. Literatura inglesa. 2. Clássicos. 3. Fantasia. 4. Imaginação. 5. Ficção científica.
I. Título. II. Série

2025-2526 CDD 823
CDU 821.111-31

Elaborada por Lucio Feitosa - CRB-8/8803
Índice para catálogo sistemático:
1 Literatura inglesa 823
2. Literatura inglesa 821.111-31

Text based on the original story by Herbert George Wells,
adapted by Gemma Barder
Illustrations by Nick Moffatt

1st edition in 2025
www.cirandacultural.com.br

THE INVISIBLE MAN

HERBERT GEORGE WELLS

W. Books

Doctor Jack Griffin

A scientific doctor

Mrs and Mr Hall

The owners of the Coach and Horses Inn

Fearenside

A train station porter

Mr Henfrey

A clockmaker

DOCTOR CUSS
A medical doctor

DOCTOR ARTHUR KEMP
A medical doctor and Griffin's university friend

MARVEL
A homeless man

COLONEL AYDE
An army colonel and Arthur Kemp's friend

Chapter One

It would be dishonest to say that Iping, a small village in the heart of West Sussex, was the most exciting place in the world. It was not even the most exciting place in England. It was a sleepy little village where people lived and worked and not very much happened at all.

Of course, all of that changed the day Doctor Jack Griffin came to stay.

At first, Mrs Hall, the landlady of the Coach and Horses Inn, saw nothing particularly odd about the man who asked to stay in a room for a week. He was wearing a heavy coat, gloves, a hat and a scarf wrapped around his head.

Over his eyes he wore a pair of dark glasses to shield him from the winter sun. She wondered if she should add a few more logs to the fire in the reception hall of the inn. Her new guest, Mr Griffin, did not take off any of his many layers while he sat waiting for his room to be made ready for him.

Once his room was prepared, Mrs Hall glanced around for the doctor's luggage. 'Can I help you with your … er … bags, sir?'

'No, no,' Griffin replied, quickly. 'I am having everything delivered to me tomorrow. It is all coming from London.'

'What a good idea,' Mrs Hall said, politely. 'Makes travelling a lot easier if you don't have to carry a lot of suitcases around with you!'

Although, she did wonder what Mr Griffin was going to do about pyjamas to sleep in – let alone a toothbrush or fresh clothes for the next day – but she did not ask any further questions. It was her job to provide a comfortable bed and a warm welcome and, as she handed Griffin his key, she was satisfied that she had done both.

When Mrs Hall returned to the ground floor of her inn and began to sweep the hall for the last time that evening, she could not help her mind from wandering back to her new guest. There seemed to be an odd emptiness to him. With his dark glasses and his scarf pulled up over his nose, she could not read the expressions on his face. *Was he content with his room or not? Was he pleased with the inn? Was he happy to be there?* She thought about it as she swept, and a strange little shiver passed down her spine.

After locking the doors of the inn for the night, she decided to check on Mr Griffin one last time, to make sure he had everything he needed. She was sure that would ease her mind a little.

'Mr Griffin?' she said, quietly, knocking gently on the door to his room. 'I'm terribly sorry to bother you, but I wanted to make sure you had everything you needed.'

'Quite sure, Mrs Hall,' came the swift reply. 'Thank you, goodnight.'

Mrs Hall smiled to herself and was about to turn away when the latch of Mr Griffin's door gave way.

She had been meaning to tighten it for weeks. The door swung open a little. She was about to apologise for the intrusion and close the door again, when she looked in and saw that, apart from the furniture, the room was completely empty.

CHAPTER TWO

The following day, Mrs Hall was furiously wiping the counter tops in the breakfast room of her inn. It was something she often did when she was angry with her husband.

'All I am saying, dearest,' said Mr Hall, as he looked over the bookings for that evening. 'Is that the room could not *possibly* have been empty. You said yourself you had just spoken to Mr Griffin and he was inside his room at the time.'

'I know what I saw!' Mrs Hall replied, crossly. 'That is, I know what I did *not* see. There was no one in that room. It was like I had been talking to a ghost!'

Mr Hall chuckled a little to himself. 'Well, if Mr Griffin has turned into a ghost, we will start to advertise ourselves as a haunted inn and double our profits!'

Mrs Hall sighed and scrubbed the counter tops even harder. At that moment, a figure walked into the room. Mr Hall smiled knowingly at his wife and said: 'Good morning, Mr Griffin! I do hope you slept well?'

Mrs Hall looked up to see Mr Griffin standing in front of her. He was wearing the same coat, hat and gloves as he had the previous day, but now Mrs Hall could see that he had removed his scarf and his face was covered in bandages.

'I slept very well, thank you,' replied Griffin. 'Although perhaps you might take a look at the latch on my door. It seems to fly open at the slightest touch.'

Mrs Hall blushed. 'I'm terribly sorry, Mr Griffin,' she said. 'I have been meaning to fix it.

Only, I could have sworn you weren't in the room …'

Mr Griffin laughed from under his bandages. 'Oh, I was there,' he said. 'Perhaps you were tired? Mr Hall, you should make your wife rest more!'

Mrs Hall's embarrassment turned to frustration. She was certain the room had been empty. She knew every inch of her hotel and there was nowhere he could have been hiding. She decided to change the subject: 'You look like you have been in the wars,' she said. 'We have an excellent doctor in Iping, I'm sure he would not mind taking a look at you.'

Griffin took a step back and gazed at the floor. 'That is very kind of you,' he said, hurriedly. 'But it is not needed. I'm afraid I have a condition that makes my skin very … sensitive. I must wear these bandages and gloves all the time.'

'Oh, I see,' Mrs Hall said, quietly. 'Well, just let me know if you need anything.'

Griffin nodded. 'Actually, Mr and Mrs Hall, there is something,' he said. 'Later this afternoon

I am expecting my luggage from London. I have quite a few boxes arriving, and I was hoping to stay at your wonderful establishment for a few more weeks to conduct some … research.'

Mr Hall straightened up, suddenly interested.

'For this, I will need not only my own room, but your parlour, too,' Griffin announced.

Mr and Mrs Hall exchanged glances. The parlour was a small room on the ground floor where guests could have a cup of tea or wait for a carriage. It was about the size of a large study, but Mrs Hall was proud that her little inn offered such a room for her guests.

'Of course, I know this is a bit of a strange request,' Griffin

continued, noticing the expression on the landlady's face. 'But I am willing to pay whatever you wish.'

Chapter Three

Despite the fact that Mr and Mrs Hall thought their inn was the best in the country, it was rarely fully booked, and it only made them just enough money to live on. So, when Mr Griffin offered to pay them double for his room and the use of their parlour, they jumped at the chance.

Just as he had predicted, Mr Griffin's boxes arrived from London that afternoon and were wheeled into the parlour by the station porter, Fearenside. After delivering the last box, Mr Griffin handed him a small tip and shut the parlour doors firmly behind him.

'Er, any idea what that fella is up to?' Fearenside asked Mrs Hall on his way out of the inn.

'None,' she said. 'Why?'

'Well, most of those cases were filled with paperwork and notebooks,' the porter replied. 'But some of them were marked

porter
A person whose job is to transport goods from one place to another.

"dangerous" and "poisonous".
Thought you ought to know.'

Fearenside's words left Mrs Hall with the same strange feeling of dread she had experienced the night before. Something wasn't quite right with Doctor Griffin. She was certain of it.

***

The following day, Mrs Hall heard strange noises coming from the parlour. She knocked on the door at lunchtime and again at dinner, to ask Mr Griffin if he would like something to eat. Both times she was told quite firmly: 'No, thank you.'

Mr Griffin did not come to the door and no other explanation was given.

The noises continued. There was rattling and bubbling. Tinkling and crackling.

Then, came the smell of gas, while wafts of smoke escaped from under the door. Mrs Hall could stand it no longer.

'Don't bother him!' said Mr Hall, trying to calm his wife's nerves.

'We've had complaints from the other guests!' said Mrs Hall. 'And besides, I want to know what is going on in there! I'm not sure all this extra money is worth it.'

At the mention of money, Mr Hall looked at his feet.

'What's the matter?' Mrs Hall asked.

'That's just it,' he said. 'Mr Griffin hasn't exactly paid us any extra money, yet.'

Mrs Hall's face flushed red. 'How much *has* he paid?'

'Well … actually … nothing.'

Mrs Hall turned and stomped her way down the corridor to the parlour door and thumped on it with her fist. 'Mr Griffin?' she called.

'No, thank you, Mrs Hall!' came the voice from inside. 'I don't want anything.'

'I'm not offering you anything!' snapped Mrs Hall, getting angrier. 'It is me who wants something from *you*!'

After a moment, the noises

stopped and the door to the parlour creaked open a tiny amount, so that Mrs Hall could only make out Mr Griffin's dark glasses. 'What can I do for you?' Mr Griffin asked, politely.

'You can pay us what you owe, or you can explain to me what is going on in there, right now!'

Chapter Four

Griffin stayed silent for a moment longer than was comfortable for either him or Mrs Hall. Eventually he cleared his throat and said: 'Of course, of course. I am sorry not to have paid you before, but my wallet was not in any of the boxes brought up from London. It will be with me in a day or two, then I can pay you everything I have promised.'

Mrs Hall's anger melted a little. Despite his strange appearance,

Mr Griffin always seemed to have an answer for every question asked. 'May I ask what exactly your "research" is, Mr Griffin?' she said. 'We've started to have complaints from the other guests.'

Griffin paused again, shifting from foot to foot. 'I do apologise,' he replied at last. 'I am a scientist and I wanted somewhere peaceful to study and conduct my experiments. If I am causing too much trouble, I can go ...'

Mrs Hall quickly weighed up in

experiments
A carefully planned test used to discover something unknown.

her mind how much Mr Griffin was offering to pay her to rent his two rooms, and how much she could stand the complaints from her other guests. The decision was clear. ‘No, no,’ Mrs Hall said, smiling politely. ‘We are happy to have you here. I’m sorry to have bothered you.’

She stepped away from the parlour feeling a little dazed and confused. She had been so angry at first, but somehow Mr Griffin had managed to make her apologise to him!

***

The following day, the local clockmaker, Mr Henfrey, came to the inn as he usually did on the first of every month. It was his job to wind and check each clock in the inn, to make sure the guests checked out on time and not a minute later.

Of course, this meant that Mr Henfrey would also have to check the clock in the parlour. Mrs Hall's curiosity was so strong that she accompanied Mr Henfrey when it was time to visit that particular room.

'Oh, Mr Griffin?' Mrs Hall called politely through the closed door. 'So sorry to disturb, but Mr Henfrey is here to wind the clocks.' No answer came from inside the parlour.

Mrs Hall tried again. 'We would not want your experiments to go wrong thanks to a slow clock, now, would we?'

After a moment, the parlour door creaked open, wide enough for Mr Henfrey and Mrs Hall to step inside. Griffin stood behind the door, in the shadows. 'Come in, come in,' he said. 'Please do what you need to do.'

Mrs Hall's eyes nearly popped out of her head when she saw that her parlour had been turned into a laboratory. Glass beakers filled with different coloured liquids were spread across every table, while charts crammed with unreadable handwriting covered the walls.

laboratory
A place used for scientific investigation and experiments.

Mr Henfrey found the clock on the mantlepiece and quickly did his work, trying not to look too shocked at the state of the room. Mr Griffin stayed in the shadows, silently watching.

'That's it,' Mr Henfrey said cheerfully, as he finished winding the clock, 'All done!'

'Thank you,' Griffin replied, quietly.

Mrs Hall watched the clockmaker leave the room, but instead of following, she stepped closer to Griffin and pulled the parlour door back slightly to take a closer look at her mysterious guest. What she saw made her step back in shock and terror. Griffin was no longer wearing his dark glasses, and where there should have been a pair of eyes, was a gaping black hole.

Chapter Five

Filled with shock and confusion, Mrs Hall left the parlour, unable to understand what she had just seen.

Or, more precisely, *not* seen.

Mr Griffin did not have a face. It simply was not there. Instead of eyes, there was the blackness of shadows and the faint impression of the parlour's wallpaper.

'No, no. It cannot be,' Mrs Hall gasped, steadying herself on the

table she used to greet her guests.

'Are you all right, Mrs Hall?' asked Mr Henfrey, as he closed his bag of tools and got ready to leave.

'I ... er ... yes, I am quite all right,' she stuttered. What else could she say? That she had just seen straight through one of her guests? 'Thank you, Mr Henfrey. Please send your bill as soon as you like, I must be getting on with my chores.'

Mr Henfrey nodded a goodbye and left the inn. For a moment all was quiet, until the door to the parlour slowly creaked open. Mrs Hall did not look. She was frightened of what she might see. She could sense the figure of Griffin walking towards her.

Still, she turned away from him.

'Mrs Hall,' Griffin began in a calm, steady voice. 'I know what you just saw might seem unsettling to you–'

'I don't know what you mean,' Mrs Hall said, quickly.

Griffin paused. 'I think you do,' he said. 'And I assure you that I am working hard to make myself well again.'

Mrs Hall felt a little queasy. Only a few moments before, she was certain she knew how the world worked. One of the things she was certain about was that people were not invisible! She straightened up, still refusing to look at him. *What should she do?* She thought. Her mind raced. She could run away, out of her inn, screaming into the streets, or she could stay calm and deal with this.

She chose to be calm.

'Two things, Doctor Griffin,' she said at last. 'One: you will agree to see Doctor Cuss. He is the doctor I mentioned when you first arrived. He is an extremely good doctor and may be able to help you.' Before Griffin could protest, she continued, 'Two:

you will pay your bill *in full* by the end of tomorrow or I shall have everything in that parlour, including you, shipped out at once!'

Silence once again fell between the two. Eventually, Griffin spoke. 'Very well,' he sighed.

Chapter Six

The following morning, Mrs Hall walked into the breakfast room of her inn to be greeted by her smiling husband. She had decided not to tell him anything about Griffin. For one thing, she was not certain he would believe her, especially not after the last time they had discussed their guest.

'You look cheerful,' she said, picking up her ledger to see which guests were arriving that morning.

'You'll be cheerful in a minute when you see what was waiting for us when I woke up this morning,' said Mr Hall, handing Mrs Hall a heavy envelope.

Taking it, she peered inside to see a huge wad of money. 'My goodness!' she gasped. 'Where did all this come from?'

'Mr Griffin,' replied Mr Hall, happily. 'It came with a note to say that should cover him until the end of the month, if we can put up with him a little longer.'

Mrs Hall flicked through the large amount of money. It was more than he had originally agreed to pay, she was sure of it. What she was not sure about, was letting Griffin stay until the end of the month.

Her thoughts were interrupted by the sound of heavy footsteps running into the inn. Fearenside stood, out of breath with one hand on his knee.

‘What on earth is the matter?’ asked Mr Hall.

‘The vicarage …’ panted Fearenside. ‘It’s been burgled!’

Mr and Mrs Hall looked at each other, amazed. Iping was the sort of village where you could leave your doors unlocked at night. Everyone knew everyone and it was safe and quiet. Mrs Hall had lived there her whole life, and this was the first time any of the homes or businesses had ever been broken into.

'What happened?' she asked in disbelief.

'That's what's so strange!' said Fearenside. 'There was no sign that anyone had broken in. The doors were locked, and

no windows were smashed. But when the vicar woke up this morning, he saw that all his money, and all the church collection from this Sunday, had been taken. It was like a ghost had slipped in and out.'

Mrs Hall's stomach churned as she glanced at the envelope full of money in her hand.

'How dreadful!' said Mr Hall. 'Do tell the vicar to come and have his dinner at the inn tonight, on us. Poor man. How have the police any hope of catching a ghost?!'

When Fearenside left, Mrs Hall asked, in a shaky voice: 'Where is Mr Griffin?'

Mr Hall gestured towards the parlour as he took the envelope of money from his wife's hands and placed it safely inside their till.

He had not made the connection between the money Mr Griffin had given him and the burglary at the vicarage – but Mrs Hall certainly had.

She went straight to the parlour

and did not bother to knock before bursting into the room. Thankfully, Griffin was covered from head to toe and was wearing his dark glasses, so she was not as afraid of him as she had been the previous day.

'It was *you*!' she said. 'You took the money from the vicarage!'

Griffin put down the beaker of purple liquid he was examining.

'Don't try to deny it,' said Mrs Hall. 'It was like a ghost, they said. A ghost!'

At that moment, the bell on the front desk rang.

‘That will be Dr Cuss for my appointment,’ Griffin said, calmly, not bothering to deny Mrs Hall’s accusations. ‘If you would not mind showing him in.’

Chapter Seven

Griffin did not move. He stared through his dark glasses at Mrs Hall. When Doctor Cuss rang the bell for a second time, she sighed with frustration and left the parlour.

'Thank goodness you have come,' she cried, taking the doctor's coat and hat. 'I am at my wit's end. I don't know what to do.'

The old doctor smoothed his grey beard and smiled at Mrs Hall.

'Now, now,' he said. 'It can't be as bad as all that. You say you have a guest staying here who needs my help?'

Mrs Hall nodded. 'He's in the parlour, he's expecting you, but he is–' Mrs Hall stopped speaking. How could she ever describe what she had seen? She decided not to. 'I shall leave you to talk to him yourself. But please be careful, Doctor Cuss.'

Doctor Cuss knocked on the parlour door and waited for

Doctor Griffin to invite him inside before entering the room. He was a little taken back by what he saw. The scientific equipment on the desk, the notes and charts all over the walls, and Mr Griffin himself, wearing his coat and gloves, his face heavily bandaged.

'Doctor Griffin?' he asked.

Griffin nodded and gestured towards two small armchairs by thc fireplace where he and the doctor could sit and talk.

'Mrs Hall tells me that I should speak to you quite urgently,' the doctor began. 'I presume this has something to do with your injuries?'

'My injuries?' Griffin replied, taking a seat opposite the doctor. 'Oh, you mean my bandages. I am not injured, doctor, but I am suffering from a … condition. I am working on a cure – as you can see. I am also a doctor, although I am a Doctor of Science.'

'You are a scientist?' the doctor asked, interested.

'I am,' Griffin replied, quietly. 'And as you can see, I am perfectly fine. I just need to be left alone to–'

'Forgive me,' the doctor interrupted. 'But you seem anything but fine. No one I know who is “fine” wears gloves and a thick woollen coat with sunglasses, inside. Perhaps I could take a look at your condition?’

Griffin shifted in his seat, uncomfortably. ‘That is quite unnecessary,’ he said, sounding a little agitated.

'Well, then at least let me take your pulse to see if your heart is okay,' the doctor said, reaching out to take Griffin's wrist. As he did so, Griffin pulled his arm away, and the sleeve of his woollen coat fell back. Where there should have been an arm was nothingness.

His sleeve stopped and there was nothing but blank space until the point where his gloved hand seemed to be floating in mid-air.

'What is this?' the doctor gasped, staring in disbelief. 'I don't understand. How can this be?'

Griffin stood up quickly and in a rage. 'Fine!' he snapped, struggling to take off his gloves to reveal an empty space where his hands should be. 'Satisfied? Why not bring the whole town to take a look?'

Chapter Eight

The doctor stood slowly. 'Mr Griffin, I admit, I have never seen anything like your "condition" before, but if you will just allow me to examine you.'

'Never!' cried Griffin. 'Be prodded and poked and put all over the newspapers? Come and "see" the Invisible Man! I will not allow it!'

The doctor tried to protest, but Griffin ignored him. He put on his gloves and left the parlour to see Mrs Hall waiting nervously a little way along the corridor.

'I will be leaving straight away, Mrs Hall,' he said. 'Please send for Mr Fearenside to gather my belongings.'

'I will do no such thing!' Mrs Hall said. 'I know who you are, and I know what you have done.'

Griffin strode towards Mrs Hall until he was so close, she could see her own reflection in his dark glasses. 'And if what you say is true, what will you do with the stolen money?' he asked, menacingly. 'Will you give it all back?'

Mrs Hall paused for a moment.

The money was more than she and her husband had seen for many months. It would pay for repairs to the inn and for firewood over the cold winter months. As she thought about what to do next, Mr Griffin laughed mockingly at her and rushed up the stairs to his bedroom.

Doctor Cuss was soon at her side, holding her arm to steady her as she swayed with the weight of what she should do.

'I can see why you did not tell me about Mr Griffin before I examined him,' Doctor Cuss said. 'But I have to admit, he is a wonder! We must be kind to the poor fellow, he seems to be in a bad way.'

Mrs Hall stared at the doctor. 'Be kind to him?!' she cried, shocked. 'Doctor, do you know what he has done? He was the one who burgled the vicarage!'

A wave of realisation crashed over the doctor's face. 'Of course,' he said, slowly, as though figuring out the whole burglary in his head. 'If he removed all his clothes, he would be completely invisible; the perfect way to get in and out of a house unseen. Simply follow them in, wait until they are asleep, steal what you like and be let out again the next morning!'

For a moment, Mrs Hall was worried that Doctor Cuss actually sounded impressed by Griffin, but the doctor soon shook off his look of amazement. 'Where is he?' he asked.

'His room,' replied Mrs Hall.

'Then I shall keep him there while you fetch the police. Hurry, Mrs Hall!'

Mrs Hall knew what she had to do, even if it meant giving back all the money. As she raced out of the inn, Doctor Cuss hurried up the stairs to Griffin's room.

'It's all over, Griffin!' called the doctor through the bedroom door.

‘We know what you have done, but perhaps now you can get the help you really need!’ When there was no reply, the doctor pushed at the door. The broken latch, which had still not been fixed, easily gave way.

Stepping inside the room, the doctor found nothing but a pile of bandages, a coat, a hat and a pair of gloves all in a heap on the floor. At first, Doctor Cuss wondered if Griffin was still in the room somewhere, until he spotted the open window.

Chapter Nine

Dr Arthur Kemp sat at his large mahogany desk, looking out of the window at the view over Harley Street in London. It was a quiet afternoon. His appointment book was empty, but he did not mind.

In fact, he was enjoying himself by reading a rather amusing story in the newspaper.

According to the news report, the sleepy village of Iping in West Sussex had been disturbed by the actions of an "invisible man". Arthur sipped his tea and chuckled to himself.

'What nonsense,' he said.

He scanned the report and took in the details. A stranger arriving in the village, a laboratory set up in an inn and a burglary at the local vicarage. Then he came to the stranger's name: Doctor Jack Griffin.

Arthur thought for a moment. The name was familiar to him, but it was a common enough name, he supposed. There was no way this ridiculous story could have anything to do with his old friend. He finished reading his newspaper, set it to one side and wandered over to the window of his study to look out over the street.

Arthur Kemp was now a respected doctor with a long list of wealthy and important patients.

Once, years ago when he was a student, he had shared a house with a group of other promising young doctors. One of these students had been called Griffin. Jack Griffin. And he had become a Doctor of Science.

It had been many years since he had seen Griffin, but he had heard about some of his experiments from friends. Although, for the last few months, no one had heard from him and it was believed that he had left the country to study abroad.

Arthur was lost in his own thoughts when he noticed a man

standing on the side of the street, staring up at his offices. The man did not look like one of his patients. He was wearing ragged, dirty clothes and had a strange look on his face.

Arthur rang for his servant, and after a moment a young footman appeared. 'Go and speak with that man,' Arthur said, gesturing to the man on the street. 'He has been watching my offices, find out what he wants and whether we can help him.'

footman

A servant whose job is to open doors and run errands around the house.

He watched from the window, as the young servant crossed the street, dodging past the carriages, to speak with the man. A long exchange occurred that Arthur could not quite work out. It was clear the man wanted something concerning Arthur's house.

Perhaps he needed a doctor and had read about him somewhere? He sometimes treated people who he knew could not afford to pay for his services and he wondered if this man was here for the same reason.

After a moment, the man followed Arthur's servant to the front door, but did not come in.

Seconds later, the footman knocked on Arthur's study door.

'Well? Who is he?' Arthur asked. 'Does he need treatment for something?'

'No, sir,' the servant replied. 'His name is Marvel. He says he has a message from a friend of yours, but he is the only one who can give it to you.'

Arthur frowned. It sounded like a story or some sort of scam to get inside the house.

'What friend?' he asked.

'He said the man's name was Doctor Jack Griffin.'

Chapter Ten

Marvel looked around Arthur Kemp's study as though he were standing in Buckingham Palace. The doctor had requested that tea and cake were brought immediately. His trained eye could see that the man was hungry and tired.

'Why don't you tell me your message,' Arthur began, 'while we wait for your refreshments?'

Marvel twisted his cap in his hands. 'Sir, I find it hard to know where to begin. I come on behalf of Jack Griffin. Do you know him?'

Arthur nodded. 'I do,' he said. 'We were good friends a long time ago. I believe he is not in the country at the moment.'

Marvel shook his head. 'Oh, he is, sir,' he said. 'He's been staying in my home village – if I can call it that when I don't actually have a house.' Marvel looked at his feet, a little ashamed. 'I suppose that's why Doctor Griffin asked me to help him. I'm the only one desperate enough and he promised to pay me.'

Arthur slowly walked over to his desk, the article about the Invisible Man was still open.

'Where did you say you were from?' he asked.

'I didn't, but I'll tell you,' replied Marvel. 'It's Iping.'

Arthur sat down heavily on his chair. He was certain now that the Jack Griffin in the newspaper was the same Jack Griffin that had once been his friend.

'He's asked if he can meet you,' said Marvel.

'Why did he not come himself?' asked Arthur. 'Or is he in this room right now? This "Invisible Man"!' Arthur laughed at the silliness of the idea, but stopped when he saw Marvel's serious face.

'Doctor Griffin was worried how you might react if he arrived unannounced,' Marvel said. 'He's a bit of an … odd looking chap.'

'So, he sent you?'

Marvel nodded.

Arthur was intrigued by everything that Marvel had told him. He was starting to believe that he was being truthful. He had not asked for any money, and he seemed serious about the job that had been given to him.

As the footman entered with

a tray of tea and some warm scones, Arthur said: 'Very well. Tell Doctor Griffin I shall see him early tomorrow morning. I have my first appointment at 10 a.m. so tell him to come at 9 a.m. Now, please, do have something to eat before the tea gets cold.'

CHAPTER ELEVEN

The following morning, Arthur Kemp got up and dressed as usual in his house on Harley Street. Although he found that he could not eat any breakfast. His mind was spinning at the thought of seeing Jack Griffin again and hearing exactly why he had been accused of disturbing a small village, and why, exactly, they called him the "Invisible Man".

He climbed the small flight of

stairs to his office, but as he got to the top and reached for the door handle, he saw that the door was already slightly open. Arthur paused. He always closed the door to his study each evening. It was his way of saying to the household that his working day was finished. Could he have forgotten? His mind had been racing after he had said goodbye to Marvel. It was possible he had been distracted.

When Arthur stepped inside, however, he immediately knew that someone else had been there. His newspaper had been moved.

The cushions on his small couch had dents in them and his window had been opened a little to let in some fresh air.

'Arthur?' came a voice.

Arthur spun round in a full circle, scanning each corner of the room. It looked empty. He was the only person there.

'It is all right, Arthur, I am not here to hurt you,' said the voice again.

'Where are you? Who is there? Come out at once!'

'I am out, Arthur,' said the voice. 'I am standing by the fireplace.'

Arthur began to tremble. Although the voice sounded like it was coming from that direction, there was no one else in the room. This had to be a cruel joke.

'It is me, Jack,' Griffin said. 'We were friends once. We studied together at–'

'I know who you are!' Arthur said, impatiently. 'But I refuse to believe that I cannot see you. Come out from wherever you are hiding!'

'I am not hiding,' Griffin replied. 'I am invisible.'

***

Arthur stoked the fire and sat opposite his empty sofa, watching in wonder as the seat cushions dented, seemingly by themselves, under the weight of the invisible man.

'Thank you,' said Griffin. 'I did not want anyone to follow me, and the only way to do that is by not wearing any clothes. As you can imagine, it gets a little chilly.'

'Would you like … that is … can you wear a blanket?' Arthur asked.

'I can,' replied Griffin, and Arthur took a woollen throw from the back of his chair and tossed it onto the sofa. He watched in amazement as the blanket rose into the air and wrapped itself around an invisible body.

'Thank you,' said Griffin. 'The truth is, I am here to ask for your help. I need to escape, but I can't do it alone.'

Arthur stayed silent for a moment or two, considering his reply. 'I will help you if I can,' he said. 'But first, you must tell me how you ended up like this.'

Chapter Twelve

'Do you remember what I was studying at university?' Griffin began.

Arthur paused, trying to remember. 'I believe it was something to do with light?' he answered.

'Yes, that is correct. Well, after we graduated, I continued my research. I wanted to see if I could change the way the eye sees things. I tried all sorts of methods, mixing different chemicals. Sometimes I turned things purple. Sometimes I turned things blue. But there was one thing I was trying to achieve above all else. Invisibility. Just think of the possibilities!

'Finally! After years of trying, I found the formula. I tried it on a piece of cloth first, and it worked. Then on a neighbour's cat, which worked so well I believe they are still looking for the poor thing.

'I refined and perfected my formula until I was certain it could be tried on a human. The trouble I have always had, Arthur, is that I am very protective of my work. I knew how important this discovery was and I did not want to risk anyone stealing my research. So, I packed everything I needed and started to move around the country from one sleepy village to another.

'Finally, I tried the formula on myself, and it worked, as you can clearly tell.'

Arthur shook his head in disbelief.

'Why didn't you come up with a cure before you tried it on yourself?' he asked.

'I thought I had, but unfortunately it did not work,' said Griffin. 'I have been this way for many months now. I must go everywhere covered in clothes and bandages, but it gets tiring. My bandages slip, my sleeves don't fall in a way that covers me completely. People always notice something. Then I arrived in Iping and I was so close to figuring out a cure that nothing else mattered.'

Arthur took yesterday's newspaper off the small table by the fire.

'It says here you stole money from a vicarage,' he said. 'Is that true?'

There was silence from the sofa.

Finally, Griffin spoke. 'Yes,' he said. 'But I was about to be thrown out of my rooms for not paying my bill. But tell me, how is it possible to earn money or go to a bank when you look the way I do? I promised myself that I would give the money back when I could.'

Arthur listened to the voice he knew so well as a student. It was the same voice of the man he had known at university, but now it was strained with desperation. He was both impressed by Griffin's discovery and appalled by his behaviour.

'What do you need me to do?' Arthur asked at last.

Griffin let out a sigh of relief. He was so grateful to his old friend that his eyes welled with tears. Arthur watched, amazed as two tiny pools of water appeared floating in the air in front of him before falling to the floor.

'Can you help me get to Spain?' Griffin asked.

Chapter Thirteen

Of course, Spain made perfect sense. It was hot most of the year, and a man like Griffin could survive unnoticed far more easily in a place where he did not have to wear heavy clothes to keep warm.

'I understand,' said Arthur. 'But have you given up hope of finding a cure?'

'No,' replied Griffin, tiredness seeping into his voice. 'But I can no longer work in England. You have read the story in the papers.'

Griffin glanced at his desk to where the news report lay. 'I confess that I have, but I thought it was a load of nonsense! I'm sure many other people will think the same.'

Arthur was suddenly aware of the shift in the air around the sofa. The cushions moved slightly, and it was clear Griffin had stood up. 'I can't risk it!' his voice said loudly. Arthur's curtains rippled slightly, indicating that Griffin was now by the window. 'Can you imagine what they would do to me if I was captured? *I* would be the science experiment – not the one conducting them.'

Arthur nodded, understanding his old friend's fears. 'Very well,

I shall help to buy you a ticket on the next ship to Spain,' he said.

Griffin laughed.

'Why would I need a ticket?' he said. 'I can walk onto any ship or train or carriage right now unnoticed.'

Arthur paused, feeling a little foolish. 'Then why do you need *my* help?'

The sofa cushions moved again and Arthur knew that Griffin was sitting opposite him once more.

'I need you to help me with two

things,' Griffin said, urgently. 'The first is to make sure Marvel sends all my research, notebooks and money to Spain once I get there. The second is, I need you to help make people afraid of me.'

Arthur stood up in shock. 'What?' he asked.

'It is the only way people will leave me alone,' Griffin answered. 'If I am discovered on my journey, I want people to be so frightened of me that they will leave me alone.'

'How on earth do you expect to do that?'

'I can do anything!' he said, excitement and desperation in his voice. 'I can steal, I can pickpocket, I can sneak up on people and hurt them – then be away before they realise anything has happened.'

Arthur shook his head. 'No, Jack, this isn't the way,' he said. 'I will help you with anything you need to leave England, but not like this.'

'It *must* be like this!' Griffin shouted. 'Help me or not. This is how it must be.'

Arthur pondered what to do next. He glanced at the clock on the mantelpiece. It was nearly 10 a.m.

'My first patient will be here in a moment,' he said.

‘I will try to help you, but you must promise not to do anything before we speak again.’

Griffin agreed and Arthur opened the door for him to leave.

Chapter Fourteen

Doctor Arthur Kemp's 10 a.m. patient just happened to be one of his very best friends. He was a colonel in the army, and he came to see Arthur at least once a month to check that he was fighting fit and ready to lead his men.

Colonel Ayde strode into Arthur's office, shaking his friend's hand, warmly. However, he soon noticed that Doctor Kemp was not his usual self.

'You look as though you've seen a ghost, my old friend!' said the jolly colonel, settling himself into the chair on the opposite side of Arthur's desk.

'It feels like I have,' Arthur replied, lowering himself slowly into his chair. 'Tell me, have you read today's newspapers?'

The colonel frowned in confusion. 'I've read *The Times*,' he replied. 'But I'm not sure what that has to do with my check-up.'

He chuckled but stopped when he saw Arthur's serious expression.

'Did you read about the burglary in Iping?' Arthur asked.

The colonel grinned. 'Oh yes! You mean the one that was done by the "Invisible Man"?' he said. 'Quite hilarious!'

At that moment, Arthur could not hold that morning's extraordinary events in any longer. He frantically told Colonel Ayde all about Griffin, and the visit he just had. He told him everything Griffin planned to do to make people afraid of him, and on hearing this, the colonel's smile faded.

'Do you mean to say this man intends to hurt people *on purpose*?' Colonel Ayde asked. 'To create some sort of fear around him so that people will leave him alone?'

Arthur nodded. The colonel stared at him for a moment before his military training took over. He began to think about how to protect the general public from this strange invisible threat.

Before Arthur could continue, both he and the colonel were distracted by a movement near the fireplace. A candlestick shifted slightly, as though it had moved all by itself.

Arthur stood up and stared wildly at the fireplace. 'Jack? Is that you?' he asked, nervously.

'Traitor!' roared Jack's voice,

filling the air of the office and almost knocking the colonel off his chair with shock. Griffin had been in the office the entire time and had not left when Arthur had opened the door for him.

'Jack ... I want to help you!' Arthur said, desperately.

'No, you don't!' replied Griffin. 'But perhaps I don't need your help. Perhaps I can make everyone afraid of me all by myself, starting now!' This time, as the study door flew open and slammed shut, it was followed by the sound of footsteps echoing down to the front door of the house. There was no question that, this time, Griffin had left.

'Doctor Kemp, I am afraid what

we have here, is a very serious situation,' said the colonel, as though he were addressing one of his men. 'I will inform the police, but we must put the word out that there is a dangerous man on the loose.'

CHAPTER FIFTEEN

On the streets, Arthur, accompanied by his footman, maid and cook, began to knock on doors and inform anyone they met that the Invisible Man was real, in London, and might be dangerous.

After informing the police, Colonel Ayde joined in the work, and soon Harley Street was filled with concerned people, nervously asking questions.

'Is he a monster?'

'What does he feed on to keep himself invisible?'

'How can we stop him if we can't see him?'

Arthur answered as many people as possible, while trying to keep them calm. Jack Griffin had once been his friend and he still could not believe he would hurt anyone. No matter what he threatened to do.

Standing apart from the noise and the chatter, Colonel Ayde spotted something. A man in a hat and dark glasses, wearing a long trench coat, was watching the crowd. As Colonel Ayde looked closer, he noticed that the coat seemed to be floating above the ground.

'Watch out!' Ayde cried, running towards the figure. 'He's here!'

The colonel began to chase Griffin. If the situation hadn't been so serious, it would have been funny to see a trench coat moving as though by itself.

'I'm warning you!' shouted Griffin, waving his arms in the air. 'Leave me alone!'

The colonel was not afraid. If he were, he would have made a very bad soldier. He glanced over his shoulder, and saw a crowd of people rushing to chase the invisible man determined to drive the danger away.

Arthur wrung his hands helplessly as the crowd gave chase. He hoped a peaceful solution could be found, but right now he couldn't see it happening.

***

It had been many weeks since Doctor Arthur Kemp had heard anything more about the invisible man who had been in his office. That fateful morning, one of Arthur's footmen had joined in with the chase. When he returned home, looking exhausted, he told his master the whole story.

The angry crowd had chased the invisible man to the river, where they were joined by

policemen. The man, or at least, the floating jacket, had leapt up onto the wall of the River Thames, and after a moment's hesitation, it was gone. A loud splash was heard and the last anyone saw of him, was his coat drifting away downstream.

Colonel Ayde was satisfied that they had driven Griffin away and shook the hand of every single person who had helped. Arthur, however, had a strange empty feeling. There was no doubt that Griffin had been troubled towards the end of his life, but he was still his friend; a friend who had been chased until he had no choice but to throw himself into the river.

For that reason, when he picked up a Spanish postcard from his doormat that morning, he felt a thrill run through him.

My dear friend,

Please excuse the theatrics of our last meeting. As you may have guessed, I threw my coat into the river to make it look as though I had fallen in. I finally made it to Spain some weeks ago and have been living here ever since. If you can bear to help me, my research notes are still under the care of Mr Marvel, whom I hope has been *trustworthy enough to keep them for me. Once I am well again, I promise you that I will send the money I stole to the vicarage in Iping.*

I hope that day will come soon.

AUTHOR BIOGRAPHY

HERBERT GEORGE WELLS

Herbert George Wells was an English author, teacher and historian, born in London in 1866. Considered by many to be the father of science fiction, Wells was so good at imagining the future that he often seems to have predicted it. His most popular stories include: *The Time Machine*, *The War of the Worlds*, *The Invisible Man* and *The Island of Doctor Moreau*.